This Book Belongs To:

_____

Keala and the Hawaiian Bird

written by Patricia McLean ❀ illustrated by Holly Braffet

BEACHHOUSE

Every fine morning, when the sun starts to rise
Over the mountains in the blue Maui sky,
Keala is woken by birds in the trees,
Greeting the day with their sweet symphony.

One chirps,

One **squawks,**

One starts to **CROW,**

And the others sing songs that Keala knows.

"Hurry, hurry," says one bird on the lānai,
"I'm up," calls Keala,
with half-open eyes.

"Who, who," asks another from under a tree.
"It's me," says Keala.
"Who else would it be!"

And even on Sunday, when Keala could rest,
The birds make sure that she's up and dressed.
With whistles and tweets and music so clear,
Keala wakes up with songs in her ear.

One **chirps**,

One

One starts to **CROW,**

And the others join in with a morning **hello!**

But one day the music just wasn't right,
And the first bird she heard was nothing she liked.

"Screee," said the bird in a noisy, high call,
"Screee," said the bird from outside the wall.

Keala jumped up and ran out the door,
But there were just birds that she'd seen before...
The one with the crown on top of his head,
The little green bird...and the one that was red.

One chirped,

One squawked,

One started to CROW,

All very nicely, in a neat little row.

Keala just laughed and rubbed sleep from her eyes,
"It's not one of you with that kind of cry!"

She looked on the roof
and up in the palm

But the noisy,
mysterious bird was just... gone!

The next day, before the sun rose in the sky,
Keala was already on the lānai.
She sat very still in a big wicker chair
And waited for bird song to fill the air.

One chirped,
One **CROWED,**
One started to **squawk,**
And soon there was music from all of the flock.

Then, "Screee," went the bird with the strange little song,
"Screee," went the bird, but not for too long.

Keala looked near the plumeria tree,
And under the hedge where that bird might be.
The only thing there was her brother's ball,
No silly bird, no, nothing at all.

The other birds twittered as Keala ran 'round,
Searching the trees and searching the ground.

One **chirped,**
One **squawked,**
One started to CROW
As Keala looked up high and down low.

"I'll find you," she said. "You can't hide for long...
Not with that silly, incredible song."

She vowed the next day she'd find that odd bird
Whose call was simply the worst that she'd heard.

So out in the yard, beneath the night sky,
She waited to hear his ridiculous cry.
On top of her tent the other birds dozed,
But Keala stayed up until the sun rose.

None chirped,
None **squawked,**
None started to **CROW,**
And Keala was worried the bird wouldn't show.

Then, "Screee," called the bird at the start of the day.
"Screee," called the bird and from not far away!

Keala crept near to the gate in the wall...

And finally saw the bird with that call.

"Tūtū!" she said, with a smile ear to ear.
"That noise...is it just your kettle I hear?"

Then Tūtū brought out a big cup of tea
And together they heard the bird symphony.

One chirped.

One **squawked,**

One started to **CROW,**

And morning arrived with a marvelous glow!

About the Author

Patricia McLean divides her time between rainy Vancouver and sunny Maui. While in Hawai'i she can often be found under the nearest palm tree with her laptop, snorkeling in Kapalua Bay, or baking coconut muffins in her kitchen. With a Master's degree in Creative Writing, she enjoys writing for both adults and tots, and spent many years creating poetry with her daughter, Erin. Her other picture book is *Keala Up a Tree.*

About the Illustrator

A graduate of Moloka'i High School, Holly Braffet has a BFA from Ringling College of Art and Design, and an MLIS from the University of Hawai'i at Mānoa. Her other BeachHouse books include *Kekoa and the Egg Mystery*, *If You Were a Dinosaur in Hawai'i*, *Maka the Magic Music Maker,* and *All Pau with Diapers.*

Copyright © 2017 by BeachHouse Publishing
Illustrations copyright © 2017 by Holly Braffet

No part of this book may be reproduced in any form or by any electronic or mechanical means, including information storage and retrieval devices or systems, without prior written permission from the publisher, except that brief passages may be quoted for reviews.
All rights reserved.

ISBN-10: 1-933067-94-2
ISBN-13: 978-1-933067-94-0
Library of Congress Control Number: 2017944670
Design by Jane Gillespie
First Printing, September 2017

BeachHouse Publishing, LLC
PO Box 5464
Kāne'ohe, Hawai'i 96744
info@beachhousepublishing.com
www.beachhousepublishing.com
Printed by RRD Shenzhen, China